The Quite Big Rock

Written by Alan Grant

Illustrated by Shalla Gray

To

Elliot Michael, Abby Rose,

Millie Maranello

And

Jonty Enzo

"There's never a dull moment with the Grays!"

Once, a long time ago,

quite a big rock sat on top of a very high mountain.

One day a tired seagull who was far from home sat on the rock to rest.

Hi! My name is Samson Seagull

The quite big rock told Samson that he was fed up.

I'm tired of being QUITE big. I want to be huge and very big.

"Well," said Samson, "I live at the seaside, and on the beach all the stones are tiny. If you went there you'd look huge and very big."

What a GREAT idea!

So the quite big rock decided to go and live by the seaside. But he had a problem: rocks can't move, can they?

He heaved... ...and he strained... ...and he tried soooo hard!

BUT HE DIDN'T EVEN BUDGE!

That night a thundercloud gathered over the top of the high mountain.
Looks like rain!
Lightning flashed.....
Thunder crashed....
WHAT A STORM!
CRASH!
WHEN SUDDENLY.....

A lightning streak flashed down –
right into the quite big rock.
It hit him so hard that some pieces
broke off – and he began to move.

Hurrah! I'm off to the seaside!

Slowly at first....

...then faster...

...and faster...

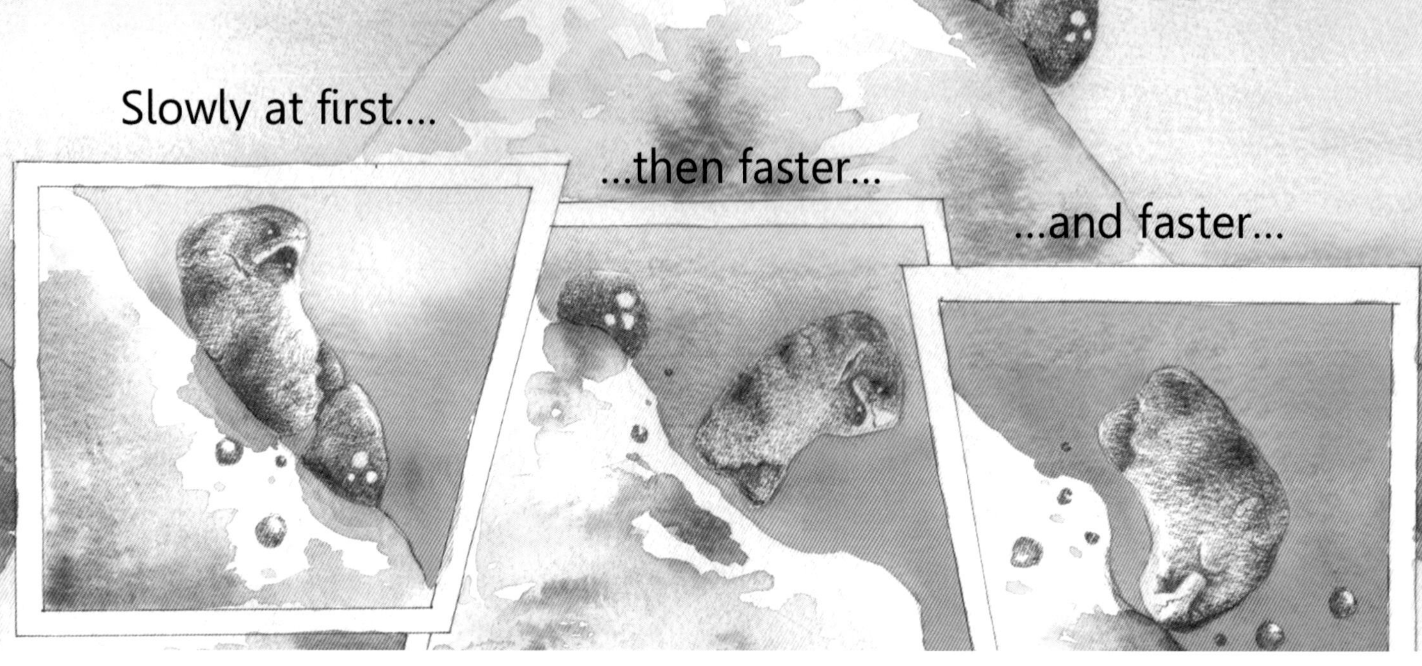

...he rolled down the mountainside, until with a mighty crash he hit a cliff.
More pieces broke off the quite big rock as his journey ended.

"Ho hum," said the rock.
"This isn't the seaside. It's nice, but I'm still only quite a big rock. Now, how do I get out of here?"

So he strained...

And he heaved...

BUT HE COULDN'T EVEN BUDGE!

But that night....there was a terrible forest fire!
Mmmm.... Things are getting hot!
A burning tree fell on to the rock.
Pieces of rock flew everywhere, but the rock didn’t mind.
The falling tree knocked him over the cliff.

Down he fell; faster...
...and faster.
THUD!
He landed with a terrific THUD and pieces of rock flew off in all directions.

He rolled over and over, until he came to rest in the middle of a stream.

He heaved...

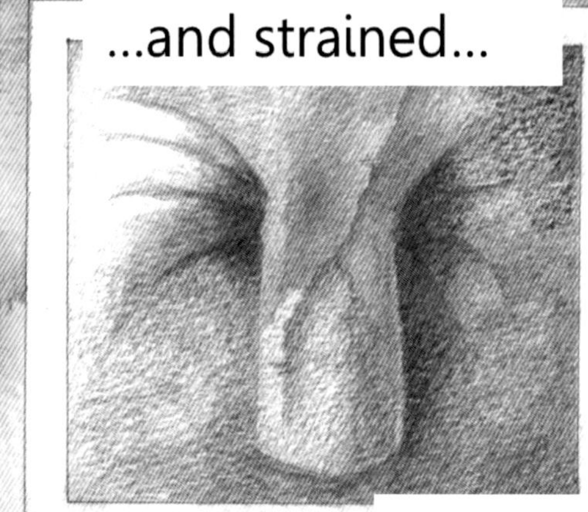

...but he couldn't budge an inch.

Then, that night, it rained and rained...
Off to the seaside again!
...and the river got fuller and fuller and deeper and deeper...
Until the water pushed the rock so hard it started to roll along underwater.
The strong current threw it against the other, bigger rocks, and the quite big rock got smaller and smaller, until at last...

He reached the sea.
ROCK
Well here I am, but where's the beach?
Just then a big wave came and threw him out on to the beach.

Samson seagull was flying by when he heard a tiny voice.
Hey, down here!
Oh hello there, Rocky
He looked down at the rock.
Ha ha ha!
I thought you said I'd be huge? But look – millions of rocks all the same size as me!
Samson nearly laughed his beak off.

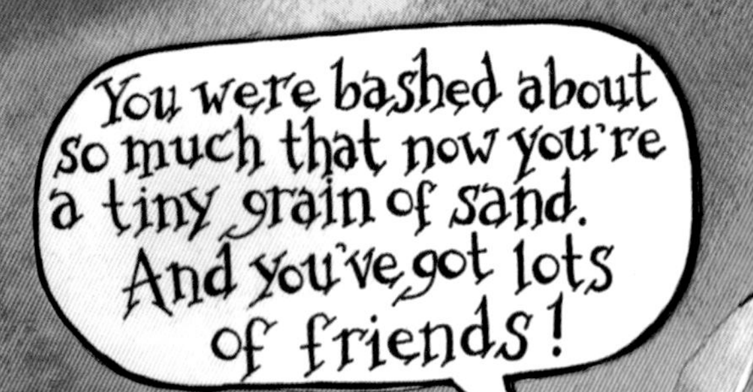

And as Samson flew off, the grains of sand (who were all once quite big rocks, and even very big rocks) sang their seaside song:

Oh I do like to be beside the seaside
Oh I do like to be beside the sea
And I'm sure that the sea would
Tell you if it could
That it likes to be – beside me!